Thi ~~...~~ **gs to:**

_____

to
ww
wwv

Published by Ladybird Books Ltd
80 Strand London WC2R 0RL
A Penguin Company
15 17 19 20 18 16 14
TEXT © LADYBIRD BOOKS LTD MCMXCVIII
ILLUSTRATIONS © ANNA C. LEPLAR MCMXCVIII

Printed in Italy

Heidi

illustrated by Anna C. Leplar

Ladybird

Once upon a time, there was a little girl called Heidi.

Heidi lived in a little town in Switzerland with her Aunt Dete. The town was near some mountains.

One day, Aunt Dete said, "Today, we will go and see your grandfather. He lives up in the mountains."

As they walked up into the mountains, they saw a boy called Peter. Peter looked after some mountain goats.

Heidi and Aunt Dete walked up to the house where Grandfather lived. Grandfather came out to meet them.

Aunt Dete said, "Heidi, I have to go to Frankfurt. You must stay here with your grandfather."

Heidi was worried. So was her grandfather. He said, "I'm much too old to look after a little girl."

But Aunt Dete went back down the mountain, and Heidi stayed with her grandfather.

"Where will I sleep?" she asked.

Grandfather made her a little bed in the hayloft. Then Peter took Heidi some goat's milk to drink.

Heidi was happy in the mountains with her grandfather. She liked the trees and flowers and she liked looking after the goats with Peter. Heidi liked the little white goat best of all. Her name was Snowflake.

13

Sometimes, Heidi went to see Peter's grandma, who was blind. Heidi told Peter's grandma about all the beautiful trees and flowers that she saw in the mountains.

But one day, Aunt Dete came back from Frankfurt.

"Heidi," she said, "it's time you went to school."

"Where must I go?" said Heidi.

"To Frankfurt," said Aunt Dete. "I will take you to stay with my friends who live there."

Grandfather was sad. "Does Heidi have to go?" he said.

Heidi was sad, too. "I want to stay here with Grandfather and Peter," she said.

But Aunt Dete said, "No. You must go to school."

Aunt Dete took Heidi to live with some of her friends in a big house in Frankfurt.

A little girl called Clara lived there. Clara could not walk. She had to stay in a wheelchair all the time.

21

Heidi liked Clara, but she wasn't happy living in Frankfurt. She wanted to go back to Grandfather and Peter in the mountains.

At night, Heidi dreamed that she was in the mountains with Snowflake, the little white goat.

One day, when Heidi came home from school, Clara said, "Last night, the maid saw a ghost on the stairs. Tonight, Daddy will stay up so that he can see the ghost, too."

So that night, Clara's father went to look for the ghost. His friend, the doctor, went with him. As they were looking, there was a noise on the stairs. It was Heidi, walking in her sleep.

"So this is the ghost, after all," said Clara's father.

The doctor took Heidi back to her bedroom.

"What were you dreaming about?" said the doctor.

"I was dreaming of the mountains," said Heidi. "I am happy here, but I miss my grandfather and Peter."

28

Clara's father was worried about Heidi. "I'll help you to go home," he said.

Heidi went to see Clara. "I will miss you when I am back in the mountains," she said.

"I will miss you, too," said Clara. "But I will come and see you one day soon."

So Heidi went back to the
mountains. Grandfather and
Peter were very happy to see her.
Peter gave her some goat's milk.
Then Heidi went to sleep in the
hayloft.

Heidi didn't walk in her sleep
that night. She was so happy
to be home.

33

The next day, Heidi went to look after the goats with Peter.

"It's wonderful to have you back," said Peter. "I missed you."

"I missed you, too," said Heidi. "I want to stay in the mountains for ever."

34

One morning, when Heidi had just got up, there was a knock at the door. It was Clara and her father.

"I have to go to town," said Clara's father. "Clara can stay here with you for a week."

Heidi was pleased to see Clara, and took her to see all the beautiful things in the mountains. But Peter was jealous of Heidi's new friend. When no one was looking, he pushed Clara's wheelchair down the mountain.

39

The next day, Clara could not find her wheelchair.

"I must try to walk," said Clara. So Heidi and her grandfather helped her to walk.

Suddenly, Clara started to walk all by herself. "This is wonderful!" said Heidi.

Peter was pleased, too. "I'm so sorry I was jealous," said Peter. "Will you be my friend, Clara?"

41

The next day, Clara's father came to take her back home. Clara walked out of the house to meet him.

"You can walk," said Clara's father. "This is the happiest day of my life."

And Heidi, Clara and Peter were friends for ever.

Read It Yourself is a series of graded readers designed to give young children a confident and successful start to reading.

Level 4 is suitable for children who are ready to read longer stories with a wider vocabulary The stories are told in a simple way and with a richness of language which makes reading a rewarding experience. Repetition of new vocabulary reinforces the words the child is learning and exciting illustrations bring the action to life.

About this book

At this stage children may prefer to read the story aloud to an adult without first discussing the pictures. Although children are now progressing towards silent, independent reading, they need to know that adult help and encouragement is readily available. When children meet a word they do not know, these words can be worked out by looking at the beginning letter (*what sound does this letter make?*) and other sounds the child recognises within the word. The child can then decide which word makes sense.

Nearly independent readers need lots of praise and encouragement.